Leo's
New Pet

Crabtree Publishing Company
www.crabtreebooks.com
1-800-387-7650

PMB 16A, 350 Fifth Ave.
Suite 3308,
New York, NY

616 Welland Ave.
St. Catharines, ON
L2M 5V6

Published by Crabtree Publishing in 2008

Series Editor: Jackie Hamley
Series Advisor: Dr. Hilary Minns
Series Designer: Peter Scoulding
Proofreader: Reagan Miller

Text © Mick Gowar 2006
Illustration © Richard Morgan 2006

The rights of the author and the illustrator
of this Work have been asserted.

First published in 2006 by
Franklin Watts (A division of
Hachette Children's Books)

Printed in the U.S.A.—CG

The author and publisher
would like to thank Robert
Kearney for permission to use
the photograph on page 4 (top)

**Library and Archives Canada
Cataloguing in Publication**

Gowar, Mick, 1951-
    Leo's new pet / Mick Gowar ;
Richard Morgan, illustrator.

(Tadpoles)
ISBN 978-0-7787-3855-8 (bound).
--ISBN 978-0-7787-3886-2 (pbk.)

    1. Readers (Primary). 2. Readers--Hamsters.
I. Morgan, Richard, 1942- II. Title. III. Series:
Tadpoles (St. Catharines, Ont.)

PE1117.T33 2008g   428.6   C2007-907416-2

**Library of Congress
Cataloging-in-Publication Data**

Gowar, Mick, 1951-
  Leo's new pet / by Mick Gowar ;
illustrated by Richard Morgan.
        p. cm. -- (Tadpoles)
  Summary: Leo's new pet hamster escapes from
its cage before Leo has even decided on a name.
  ISBN-13: 978-0-7787-3855-8 (reinforced lib. bdg.)
  ISBN-10: 0-7787-3855-8 (reinforced lib. bdg.)
  ISBN-13: 978-0-7787-3886-2 (pbk.)
  ISBN-10: 0-7787-3886-8 (pbk.)
  [1. Hamsters--Fiction.] I. Morgan, Richard Charles,
1966- ill. II. Title.
  PZ7.G747Le 2008
  [E]--dc22
                                                2007049217

Leo's New Pet

by Mick Gowar

Illustrated by Richard Morgan

Crabtree Publishing Company

www.crabtreebooks.com

Mick Gowar

"My daughter Frances had a hamster called Peanut who escaped. He was coaxed back into his cage with peanuts!"

Richard Morgan

"I hope you enjoy reading this story as much as l enjoyed drawing Leo and his dad looking for that cheeky hamster."

Leo had a new pet —
a tiny hamster.

He didn't have
a name.

"We'll give him a name
tomorrow," said Dad.

"We'll see him in the morning," said Dad.

"He's gone!" cried Leo.

"No," said Leo.

"He's under the
couch."

"Call him," said Dad.

"But he hasn't got
a name," said Leo.

"Will he come
out for a carrot?"

"No," said Leo.

"Let's try peanuts,"
said Leo.

"I know what to call him," said Leo.

"Peanut!"

Notes for adults

TADPOLES are structured to provide support for early readers. The stories may also be used by adults for sharing with young children.

Starting to read alone can be daunting. **TADPOLES** help by providing visual support and repeating high frequency words and phrases. These books will both develop confidence and encourage reading and rereading for pleasure.

If you are reading this book with a child, here are a few suggestions:

1. Make reading fun! Choose a time to read when you and the child are relaxed and have time to share the story.

2. Talk about the story before you start reading. Look at the cover and the blurb. What might the story be about? Why might the child like it?

3. Encourage the child to reread the story, and to retell the story in their own words, using the illustrations to remind them what has happened.

4. Discuss the story and see if the child can relate it to their own experiences, or perhaps compare it to another story they know.

5. Give praise! Children learn best in a positive environment.

If you enjoyed this book, why not try another TADPOLES story?

At the End of the Garden
9780778738503 RLB
9780778738817 PB

Bad Luck, Lucy!
9780778738510 RLB
9780778738824 PB

Ben and the Big Balloon
9780778738602 RLB
9780778738916 PB

Crabby Gabby
9780778738527 RLB
9780778738831 PB

Five Teddy Bears
9780778738534 RLB
9780778738848 PB

I'm Taller Than You!
9780778738541 RLB
9780778738855 PB

Leo's New Pet
9780778738558 RLB
9780778738862 PB

Little Troll
9780778738565 RLB
9780778738879 PB

Mop Top
9780778738572 RLB
9780778738886 PB

My Auntie Susan
9780778738589 RLB
9780778738893 PB

My Big, New Bed
9780778738596 RLB
9780778738909 PB

Pirate Pete
9780778738619 RLB
9780778738923 PB

Runny Honey
9780778738626 RLB
9780778738930 PB

Sammy's Secret
9780778738633 RLB
9780778738947 PB

Sam's Sunflower
9780778738640 RLB
9780778738954 PB